SIMON SPOTLIGHT

An imprint of Simon & Schuster Children's Publishing Division
1230 Avenue of the Americas, New York, New York 10020
This Simon Spotlight hardcover edition August 2017

SIMON SPOTLIGHT and colophon are registered trademarks of Simon & Schuster, Inc.
For information about special discounts for bulk purchases, please contact Simon & Schuster Special
Sales at 1-866-506-1949 or business@simonandschuster.com.
Manufactured in China 0617 SCP
10 9 8 7 6 5 4 3 2 1
ISBN 978-1-5344-0451-9 (hc)
ISBN 978-1-5344-0452-6 (eBook)

CHALK IT UP
Imagine That!

By Cala Spinner
Interior illustrations by Erin Gallagher

Simon Spotlight
New York   London   Toronto   Sydney   New Delhi

Amazing things are happening all around town everywhere you look. Do you want to see?

$4 \times 4 = 16$

Mayday! Mayday! There are creatures on the loose!
Look out below!

Look up above!

Best friends Zoey, Connor, and Grace are deep-sea explorers on a very important mission! Did a mermaid just glide by?

Taylor and Logan love movies set in space, but they love something else even more—*going* to space! Watch for shooting stars!

What's this? An incredible shrinking machine has just arrived in Emily and Noah's driveway.

Whatever you do, Noah, do *not* press that button. It's too risky! The machine has never been tested before!

Too late . . .

Something very mysterious has happened to the playground . . . it has turned into a pirate ship! *Aaaargh!* Shiver me timbers.
Being a pirate is fun!
But be careful. That's not a diving board.
It's a plank!

Marvelous things are happening at Daniel and Sophia's house, too. The forks are dancing! An apple is singing! The cookies are swimming! And what are those spoons up to?

Isabella is the star of the show!

And Ethan might be running to the bus . . . or he might be winning a marathon!

FINISH LINE

These best friends have gone inside their favorite video game.
It's time to level up!

Hear ye, hear ye! Now presenting Prince Milo and Princess Ava—of the backyard!

On no! Someone let the dinosaur out of the preschool again!
Everybody, run!

Look around you. What can you see? Can you imagine what else it could be? Can you imagine what else *you* could be?

With a little bit of chalk and a lot of imagination, anything is possible!